First published in Great Britain in 1990
by Simon & Schuster Young Books
Reprinted in 1992 and 1994

Reprinted in 1995 and 1997
by Macdonald Young Books
61 Western Road
Hove
East Sussex
BN3 1JD

Photoset in Souvenir Light
Colour origination by Scantrans Pte Ltd, Singapore
Printed in Belgium by Proost International Book Production

British Library Cataloguing in Publication Data
Forsyth, Anne
    The laughing snowman
    I. Title II. Lambert, Thelma
    823'.914[J]

ISBN 0 7500 0252 2

Anne Forsyth

THE LAUGHING SNOWMAN

Illustrated by Thelma Lambert

MACDONALD YOUNG BOOKS

Chapter One

"We'll have snow before long," said Dad,
looking up at the sky.

"Snow," said Mum, and she shivered.

"Snow," said Emma's sister Mandy. "Well,
I won't go out. I'll stay indoors by the fire."

"Snow!" said Emma. "We haven't had snow
for years!"

All day at school, she kept looking out of
the window, watching for the first snowflakes.
It got colder and colder, but still it didn't snow.

That night when she snuggled down under
the duvet, Emma meant to stay awake – just in
case it snowed during the night. But in ten
minutes she was fast asleep.

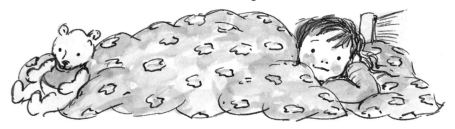

When she woke up next morning, she knew right away that something had happened. There was a strange silence. Usually she could hear the rumble of traffic in the distance. Often there was the sound of a car engine spluttering into life across the way. But this morning it was very quiet.

Emma jumped out of bed and flung open the curtains.

All over the garden was a soft downy covering of pure white. Snow hung like icing sugar along the branches of the tree by the gate.

She ran through to wake up Mum and Dad. "It's snowed! Get up! Look!"

"Mmm . . ." said Dad.

"Uh-huh," said Mum.

They didn't seem a bit interested. So she went to tell Mandy.

"Go away," Mandy mumbled sleepily. "It's Saturday."

Of course it was! No school! Emma began to make all sorts of plans. She and her friend Becky, who lived next door, could have a wonderful day. Perhaps they could go sledging in the park. She began to get dressed as quickly as she could.

"No," said Mum a little later. "You are not going out without a proper breakfast."

By now, the family was beginning to get up.

"I'd better clear the front path and put down salt, in case it freezes tonight," said Dad.

"I'll brush the snow off the shrubs, or the weight will break the branches," said Mum.

"I'll feed the birds," said Emma.

"Well, I'm not going out," said Mandy. "I've got a great book to read, all about the jungle."

"Look!" said Mum. "Someone's enjoying the snow." Sooty the cat was walking down the path. His paw prints led from a gap in the hedge, so you could see he had been visiting the house next door.

"Now can I go out?" said Emma, swallowing her last drop of coffee.

"Wrap up well," said Mum. So Emma put on her anorak and boots and wound a thick scarf round her neck. Then she gathered up the scraps of food to feed the birds.

She squeezed through the gap in the fence and went next door to Becky's house. Becky was just as excited to see the snow.

"What shall we do first?"

"I know," said Emma. "Let's build a snowman."

"Let's build *two* snowmen," said Becky. "One by your door and one by mine."

So they began.

"I've got a brilliant idea," said Becky. "But I'm not telling you what it is."

They started building the snowmen on either side of the fence. First they made the bodies, then rolled snowballs to make the round heads on top.

They didn't speak very much but kept glancing across at each other's work.

Emma found some round stones to make buttons down the snowman's front, and added more stones for his eyes and teeth, so that it looked as if the snowman's mouth was open.

But she hadn't finished yet. She went indoors. Mandy was reading, and she didn't even look up.

"You can come and help with my snowman if you like." Emma felt very good and unselfish as she said this. After all, the hard work had been done. Dressing the snowman was much more fun.

"No, thanks." Mandy drew closer to the fire. "I'd like to live in a place where it was really hot, where there were all sorts of strange plants and reptiles and beautiful humming birds."

"But it's snowed . . ."

"Yeah," said Mandy, and went on reading about the giant ant eater in the steamy swamps of South America.

"Mum, I need an old hat and scarf . . ."

"There's a box for the school jumble. There might be something in there . . ." Mum was busy and not really listening.

Emma found an old scarf of Dad's and a battered hat.

Outdoors, she tied the scarf round the snowman's neck and put the battered old hat on his head.

It looked really good.

"I've a much better idea," said Becky.

She disappeared indoors and came back carrying a clown's hat and a ruff for his neck and a red plastic nose. Then Emma remembered – Becky's brother Ben had dressed as a clown at a fancy dress party. He'd worn baggy trousers and the colourful hat and the ruff.

Becky put the hat on the snowman's head and the ruff round his neck. She put stones for the eyes and mouth then pushed the red bobble of a nose into the centre of his face.

"Great," said Emma.

"Brilliant," said Becky proudly.

Chapter Two

On Monday at school, everyone had stories to tell about sledging and snowball fights and the fun they'd had in the snow. No one wanted to talk about anything else.

That afternoon Emma's grandad called in for a cup of tea while he waited for the bus home. When Emma returned from school, there was Grandad smiling and full of jokes as usual.

"Hallo there!" he said. "That's a fine snowman at your door. All your own work? I know a good joke about a snowman – you won't have heard this one . . ."

It began to snow again and Mum turned on the radio.

"You won't be able to get home," she said to Grandad. "The road's blocked. The buses can't get through. You'll just have to stay here."

So Grandad rang up Gran and told her not to worry. "If I can't get home, I might as well make myself useful," he said with a grin. "Any odd jobs I can do?"

In the middle of the night Emma woke up and wondered what would happen if they were snowed in. Maybe she wouldn't be able to get to school.

She was just about to turn over and go back to sleep, when she heard a strange sound. It was like someone laughing – a deep, jolly sort of laugh.

It was very quiet in the house – everyone was asleep. There was no sound except for the ticking of the landing clock and the tap-tap of the bare stems of a climbing rose against the window. And that strange laugh.

Now there was another sound. Emma could hear purring. She knew that sound very well: it was Sooty, who liked to wander round the house at night, in search of company.

"Good old puss," whispered Emma. "Can *you* hear anything?" But Sooty only purred louder at the sound of a friendly voice.

"Ha! Ha!" There it was again. There *was* someone laughing.

Emma tiptoed through to tell Mum and Dad. "Listen, there's someone laughing."

"Mmm? Go back to bed, Emma. It's only a dream."

Mandy was dreaming that she was an explorer in the tropics, and she'd just found a strange wild bird on the shores of a desert island.

It had a huge bill and long, wispy feathers.

"Maybe," she thought, "I've discovered the dodo. But it's extinct. It used to live years and years ago, and it's died out, the dodo. Oh! Oh!"

"Oh! Oh!" said a voice in her ear.

Mandy woke up with a start. Emma was standing by her bed, her hair all messy and her eyes wide.

"Ho, ho!" she said. "Can't you hear it?"

"Wassermatter?" said Mandy sleepily.

"Someone laughing. Ha! Ha! Ho! Ho!"

"You woke me up," said Mandy crossly. "You're dreaming. Go back to bed."

She humped herself under the bedclothes and tried to return to her dream. But the dodo had disappeared. She wasn't on a wild tropical island any more but in her own bed in the middle of a cold January night.

Emma wondered if she should wake Grandad. She decided not to. She would find out for herself what was happening.

She crept very quietly downstairs into the kitchen and drew aside the curtain. It was bright moonlight and she could see quite clearly.

There was the snowman standing by the fence. And he was laughing. His round head rocked from side to side. "*Ho! Ho!*"

Then suddenly, just
as if he knew someone
was watching, he
stopped laughing and
stood quite still.

Emma hardly dared
move. She watched
for a little longer
but nothing happened.
So she crept back
to bed.

In the morning, she thought she must have
dreamt it. But she felt so sure she had heard the
snowman laugh.

"Anything wrong?" asked Mum. "You're very
quiet this morning."

"Just thinking," said Emma.

"That makes a change," said Mandy.

"Now, now," said Mum. "No squabbling this
early in the morning."

"Wasn't me started it," said Mandy. She still hadn't forgiven Emma for waking her from her wonderful dream. Just think, she might have discovered what had happened to the dodo. People said that sailors long ago hunted the dodo as food, and pigs and dogs and other animals took the dodo's eggs. So it couldn't survive. But just suppose it was still somewhere and she, Mandy, went on its trail! She picked up her book.

"And don't read at the table, I've told you before," said Mum.

Mandy sighed. How was she ever going to be a great explorer if people kept on and on about silly things? She was sure great explorers like Columbus and Marco Polo didn't have little sisters and bossy mothers.

Emma couldn't wait to tell Becky about the snowman. But Becky didn't believe her. "I think you dreamt it."

"No, I didn't – honest."

All that day Emma couldn't think of anything
else. She decided to ask her teacher.

"What would make a snowman laugh?"

"I don't know," she said. "I give up. What
would make a snowman laugh?"

"I don't know either," said Emma.

"Oh, I thought it was another of your jokes,"
said the teacher. "Will you give out these work
sheets for me?"

Chapter Three

Grandad was still staying with Emma's family. He was sure to know. Grandad knew everything – or nearly everything.

When she got home, Emma asked Grandad, "Do you know what makes a snowman laugh?"

"Don't know that one," said Grandad. "You've caught me there."

He went on: "Did I ever tell you about the time our whole village was snowed up in 1947?"

He told Emma how lots of small villages far from main roads were snowbound for weeks and how planes dropped bales of hay to the farms to feed the cattle.

Maybe someone else would know, thought Emma. When she went along to the shops with Mum that afternoon, she asked her friend the newsagent, "Do you know what makes a snowman laugh?"

"What's that?" The newsagent lifted a pile of evening papers on to the counter and slit the string around them. "I'll tell you something," he smiled. "When I first came to England I was just your age. I'd never seen snow. I was so excited I'll never forget. Now, of course, I don't get so excited about it. It means late deliveries, paper boys can't get here, that sort of thing."

That night, Emma was determined to find out just what had made the snowman laugh. She got into bed and put her alarm clock under the pillow, setting it for midnight, when everyone else in the house would be asleep.

She put her jersey and trousers and anorak by the bed so that she could get dressed quickly.

It seemed she had hardly closed her eyes before the alarm began to ring.

She switched it off and groped for the bedside light. Then she jumped out of bed and put on her jersey and trousers and anorak over her pyjamas. She took the torch she'd been given for Christmas and crept downstairs into the kitchen.

She stopped and listened. Yes, there it was, that jolly laugh. "*Ha! Ha!*"

She had to find out what was making the snowman laugh.

She had just grasped the handle of the back door, when a voice behind her said, "What are you doing downstairs at this time of night?"

Emma whirled round. Grandad stood in the doorway, his hair all rumpled. He was wearing his coat over the pyjamas he'd borrowed from Dad.

"I thought I heard something," he said.

"It's my snowman – he's laughing," whispered Emma.

"Laughing?" Grandad chuckled. "That's a good one . . ."

"Look! You can see for yourself."

So Grandad unlocked the back door and peered out.

"See," he said. "There's nothing there. You dreamt it . . ."

"I didn't," said Emma. "Look!" She pointed to the snowman who was rocking backwards and forwards. Just across the fence stood Becky's snowman clown. But he wasn't standing still.

He was juggling with three snowballs. Every
now and then he would drop one on the
ground. Then Emma's snowman laughed even
harder.

"He's juggling!" said Emma.

The snowman threw
first one, then two,
then three snowballs
into the air and
tried to catch them.
They fell with a
plop on his head,
on his nose and on
the ground.

Emma's snowman laughed again and the
other snowman joined in. "*Ha! Ha! Ha!*"

Emma began to
laugh too, but as
soon as they heard
her, both snowmen
stood quite still
like blocks of ice.

Emma and Grandad looked at each other
and smiled.

"Well, now," said Grandad, as they went
upstairs again. "Well, well . . ."

Chapter Four

Next morning, Emma didn't say anything about
the snowman to Mum or to Mandy. Dad had
left for work and Grandad wasn't up yet. But
she could hardly wait to rush next door and tell
Becky. Becky was furious that she'd missed the
juggling snowman. After all, it was *her*
snowman. But she slept at the back of the
house and hadn't heard a thing.

"It's true, really it is," said Emma.

"All right. I'll watch tonight," said Becky.

But that day the sun shone and it wasn't so cold. Little by little, the snow began to melt.

Sooty's pawmarks in the snow got larger as the snow melted, as if a lion or a puma had walked across the grass.

"Slush next," said Mum. "But at least it's warmer."

"Slush – ugh," said Mandy. But she didn't even look out of the window. She was going to write to the author of her book about the jungle, and ask if she could join one of his expeditions when she was a bit older.

"Slush," said Grandad. "Well, I expect the road will be open now. I'd better be getting home. Thank you for having me to stay."

"Grandad," said Emma in a low voice when they were alone together, "wasn't that fantastic – about the snowman and the juggling? No one would believe us if we told them."

"A lot of funny things happen when it snows,"
said Grandad, and he winked.

Look out for more titles in the Yellow Storybooks series:

Tell Tale Tom by Anne Forsyth

Tom loved making up tall stories – even though they always got him into all sorts of trouble!

The Excitement of Being Ernest by Dick King-Smith

The other dogs in Ernest's village aren't a very friendly bunch. They all look down their well-bred noses at poor Ernest, who doesn't even know what kind of dog he is!

Emily's Legs by Dick King-Smith

At first, nobody noticed Emily's legs. Then, at the Spider Sports, everyone began to ask questions.

Sir Garibald and Hot Nose by Marjorie Newman

Sir Garibald and his dragon Hot Nose need some money. So they devise a cunning scheme that doesn't go quite to plan...

Princess Sophie's Quest by Jacqui Farley

Princess Sophie thinks it will be easy peasy to rescue a prince. But all the silly princes she meets refuse to be rescued. Surely there's a prince in danger *somewhere*.

Storybooks are available from your local bookshop or can be ordered direct from the publishers. For more information about storybooks write to: *The Sales Department, Macdonald Young Books, 61 Western Road, Hove, East Sussex BN3 1JD.*